Dragonflies

Joi Washington

You can see the dragonfly with the eyes.

You can see the dragonfly with the hair.

You can see the dragonfly with the legs.

You can see the dragonfly with the wings.

You can see the dragonfly with the flower.

You can see the dragonfly with the leaf.

You can see the dragonfly with the grass.

You can see the dragonfly with the stick.

You can see the dragonfly with the water.

You can see the dragonfly with the rock.

You can see the dragonfly with the bee.

You can see the dragonfly with the moth.

You can see the dragonfly with the bird.

You can see the dragonfly with the spider.

Power Words
How many can you read?

You

you

can

see

the

with